50 Hilarious Knock-Knock Jokes for Kids!

By Emilia Marshall

Knock, knock.

> Who's there?

Who!

> Who who?

That's what an owl says!

Knock, knock.

> Who's there?

Lettuce!

> Lettuce who?

Lettuce in, it's cold out here.

Knock, knock.

Who's there?

Wooden shoe!

Wooden shoe who?

Wooden shoe like to hear another joke?

Knock, knock.

Who's there?

Cow says!

Cow says who?

No silly, a cow says Mooooo!

Knock, knock.

Who's there?

Atch!

Atch who?

Bless you!

Knock, knock.

Who's there?

I am!

I am who?

You don't know who you are?

Knock, knock.

Who's there?

Ya!

Ya Who?

Wow, I'm excited to see you too.

Knock, knock.
  Who's there?
Boo!
  Boo who?
Don't cry, it's just me.

Knock, knock.
  Who's there?
Avenue!
  Avenue who?
Avenue knocked on this door before?

Will you remember me in 2 minutes?
    Yes.
Knock, knock.
    Who's there?
Hey, you didn't remember me!

Knock, knock.
    Who's There?
Barbie!
    Barbie Who?
Barbie Q Chicken!

Knock, knock.

Who's there?

Turnip!

Turnip who?

Turnip the volume, it's quiet in here.

Knock, knock.

Who's there?

Ice cream!

Ice cream who?

Ice cream if you don't let me in!

Knock, knock.

Who's there?

Cow-go!

Cow-go who?
No, Cow go MOO!

Knock, knock.
Who's there?
Water
Water who?
Water you doing in my house?

Knock, knock
Who's there?
Beef!
Beef who?
Before I get cold, you'd better let me in!

Knock, knock.
     Who's there?
Leaf!
     Leaf Who?
Leaf Me Alone!

Knock, knock.
     Who's there?
Tank!
     Tank who?
You're welcome!

Knock, knock.
Who's there?
Howard!
Howard who?
Howard I know?

Knock, knock.
Who's there?
Abe!
Abe who?
Abe C D E F G H...

Knock, knock.

Who's there?

Cash!

Cash who?

No thanks, but I'd like some peanuts

Knock, knock.

Who's there?

Alpaca!

Alpaca who?

Alpaca the trunk, you pack the suitcase!

Knock, knock.

Who's there?

Alma!

Alma who?
Alma not going to tell you!

Knock, knock.
Who's there?
Ken!
Ken who?
Ken I come in, it's freezing out here?

Knock, knock.
Who's there?
Pizza!
Pizza who?
Pizza really great guy!

Knock, knock.
    Who's there?
Justin!
    Justin who?
Justin time for dinner!

Knock, knock.
    Who's there?
Isabelle!
    Isabelle who?
Isabelle broken? That's why I knocked!

Knock, knock.
    Who is there?

Teddy!
Teddy who?
Teddy is the first day of school!

Knock, knock.
Who's there?
Canoe!
Canoe who?
Canoe help me with my homework?

Knock, knock.
Who's there!
B-4!
B-4 who?
B-4 you go to school, do your homework!

Knock, knock.
>Who's there?
Stay!
>Stay who?
Stay home from school if you feel ill.

Knock, knock.
>Who's there?
I love!
>I love who?
You forgot who you love?

Knock, knock.
    Who's there?
Howard!
    Howard who?
Howard you like a big hug!

Knock, knock.
    Who's there?
Abby!
    Abby who?
Abby birthday to you!

Knock, knock.
   Who's there?
Stopwatch!
   Stopwatch who?
Stopwatch your doing and have a happy birthday!

Knock, knock.
   Who's there?
A door!
   A door who?
A-door-able me wishing you a happy birthday!

Knock, knock.
    Who's there?
Holly!
    Holly who?
Holly-days are here again!

Knock, knock.
    Who's there?
Mary!
    Mary who?
Mary Christmas!

Knock, knock.
    Who's there?
Donut!
    Donut who?
Donut open till Christmas!

Knock, Knock!
　　Who's there?
Ben!
　　Ben who?
Ben waiting for Halloween all year!

Knock, Knock!
　　Who's there?
Will!

Will who?
Will you let me in? It's freezing out here!

Knock, Knock!
> Who's there?

Icy!
> Icy who?

Icy what you are doing!

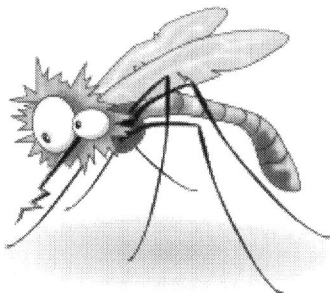

Knock, Knock!
> Who's there?

Snow.
> Snow who?

Snow use. I forgot my name again!

Knock, knock!
  Who's there?
Gorilla!
  Gorilla who?
Gorilla me a cheese sandwich.

Knock, knock!
  Who's there?
Amos.
  Amos who?
A Mosquito bit me.

Knock, knock!
Who's there?
Goat!
Goat who?
Goat to the door and find out.

Knock, Knock!
Who's there?
A herd!
A herd who?
I herd you were home, so I came over!

Knock, Knock!
Who's there?
Ice Cream Soda!
Ice Cream Soda who?
Ice cream soda whole world will hear.

Knock Knock!
 Who's there?
Broccoli!
 Broccoli who?
Broccoli doesn't have a last name, silly.

Knock, Knock!
 Who's there?
Eat!
 Eat who?
Eat your veggies!

THE END

HAPPY HOLIDAYS!

Printed in Great Britain
by Amazon